Moonbeam

The Little Elephant

written by **Dr. G. Sivakumar**
illustrated by **N. Karunakar**

IDREAM Publications, Inc./Pennsylvania

In a faraway land, there was a big, beautiful jungle. It was green all over and filled with beautiful, sweet-smelling flowers. In that jungle lived a family of elephants: Arthur, Irma, and their baby, Moonbeam.

The elephants played all day in the warm, golden sunshine.
At night they slept under a sky filled with sparkling, silver stars.

They took long baths in the river.
Arthur and Irma used their trunks to scoop up water.
Then they showered it over little Moonbeam.

They chewed juicy leaves from the tall trees. They ate fresh, sweet sugarcane from the sugarcane grove. Moonbeam loved sugarcane – it was her favorite.

The three of them lived very
happily in the jungle, until...

One day, a hunter noticed the elephants from a distance. The hunter thought to himself, "I could trap that baby elephant and sell her for a lot of money!"

So the hunter watched…

Later that day, as Moonbeam played in the jungle, her parents went to the sugarcane grove to get Moonbeam's favorite food.

The hunter saw Moonbeam all alone and knew it was his best chance to capture her. He began to set a trap. He dug a deep pit in the ground, not far from where Moonbeam was playing.

When he finished digging, he covered the pit with branches and leaves to hide it.

Then the hunter waited…

Moonbeam looked forward to the sweet sugarcane her mom and dad were bringing for her. She trotted gleefully through the vines and leaves on the jungle floor.

The little elephant didn't see the hole beneath the branches and leaves. She fell right into the pit! The hunter jumped out from his hiding place and tied Moonbeam with his rope. She was very afraid.

The hunter drove Moonbeam out of the jungle. Far from her home he hid her in a place in the city where no one could find her.

There, he kept little Moonbeam.
"I'll sell you for a very nice price!"
he said to the little elephant, smiling.
Tears streamed from Moonbeam's eyes.

Arthur and Irma returned from the sugarcane grove, trumpeting to their little baby. Moonbeam did not reply. Closer and closer they came, calling to Moonbeam with each step. Still, there was no answer from their baby.

Arthur and Irma were very worried and began searching for Moonbeam. They shook the trees with their trunks. They pounded the ground with their large feet. Moonbeam did not answer. Arthur and Irma asked every animal they passed if it had seen their baby. They asked the cheetahs, the giraffes, and the baboon… they even asked the lions. No one had seen Moonbeam.

Many weeks passed, yet Arthur and Irma did not give up their hope of finding little Moonbeam. Each day they searched until long after sunset. As soon as the sun rose, they looked for their little baby again.

One day, when Arthur
was searching for Moonbeam,
he heard a voice cry out:
"Help! Help me, I'm sinking!"

Arthur began looking for the voice and came to a clearing. There he saw a hunter trapped in quicksand. The man was slowly sinking into the loose sand and water.

Arthur quickly held out his trunk and the hunter grabbed on to it. Arthur used his great strength to pull the man from the quicksand and saved his life.

The hunter was so grateful.
He thanked Arthur over and over again.

The hunter understood that Arthur was
Moonbeam's father, because he had seen them play.
The man was ashamed because of what he had done.

He rubbed the great elephant on the trunk and said, "Dear friend, there is something I want to do for you. I would not be alive, if it were not for you."

The hunter turned and walked toward the city.
"I will be back soon; please, wait here."

Although Arthur was not sure what to expect, he waited in the clearing. Shortly after, Irma came to join him. They stood there together awaiting the hunter's return.

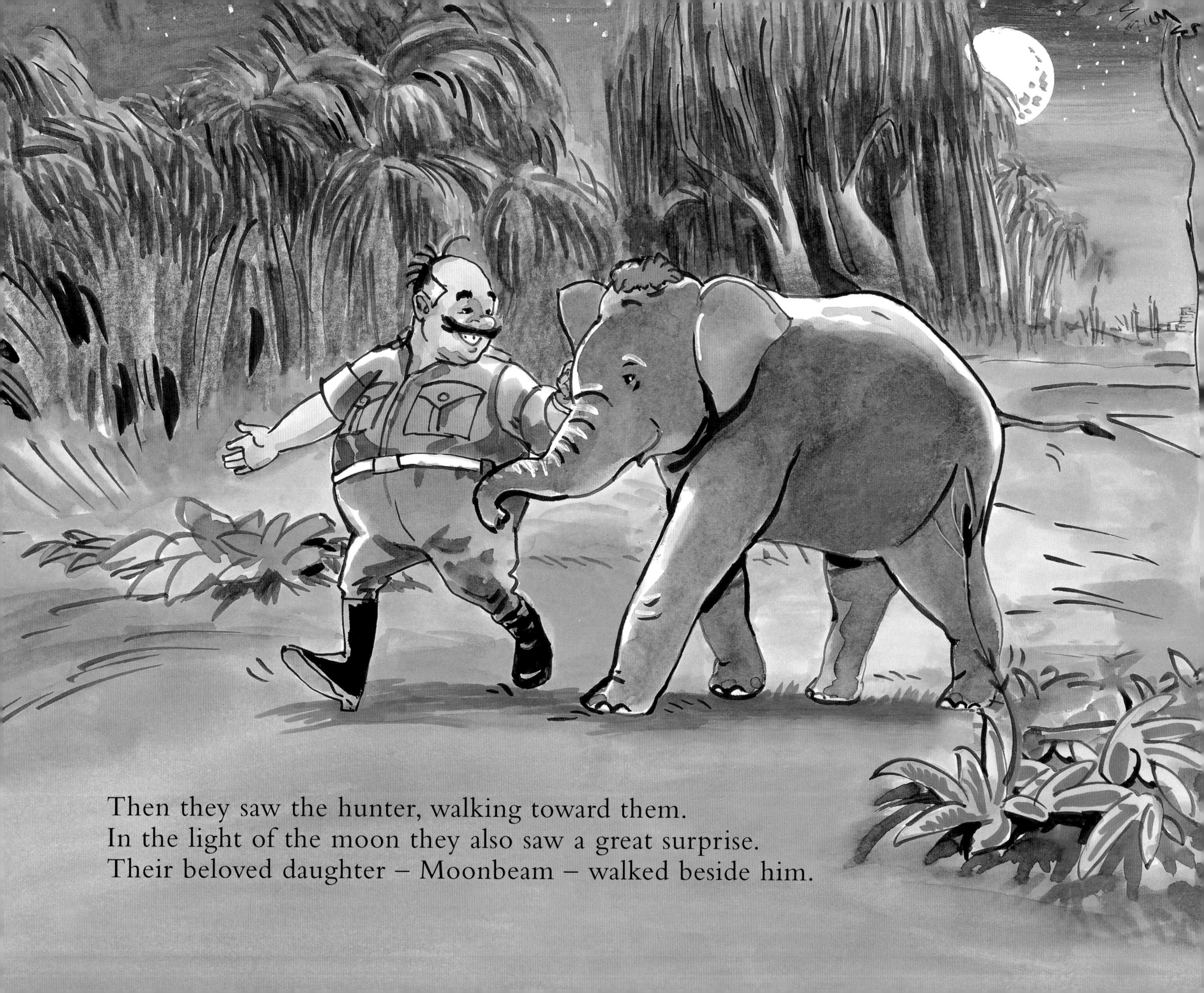

Then they saw the hunter, walking toward them.
In the light of the moon they also saw a great surprise.
Their beloved daughter – Moonbeam – walked beside him.

When Moonbeam saw her parents she let out a cry of joy. Arthur and Irma could not believe their eyes. "Moonbeam!" they both trumpeted.

They ran to their baby and hugged her.
The elephant family shed many tears of joy.

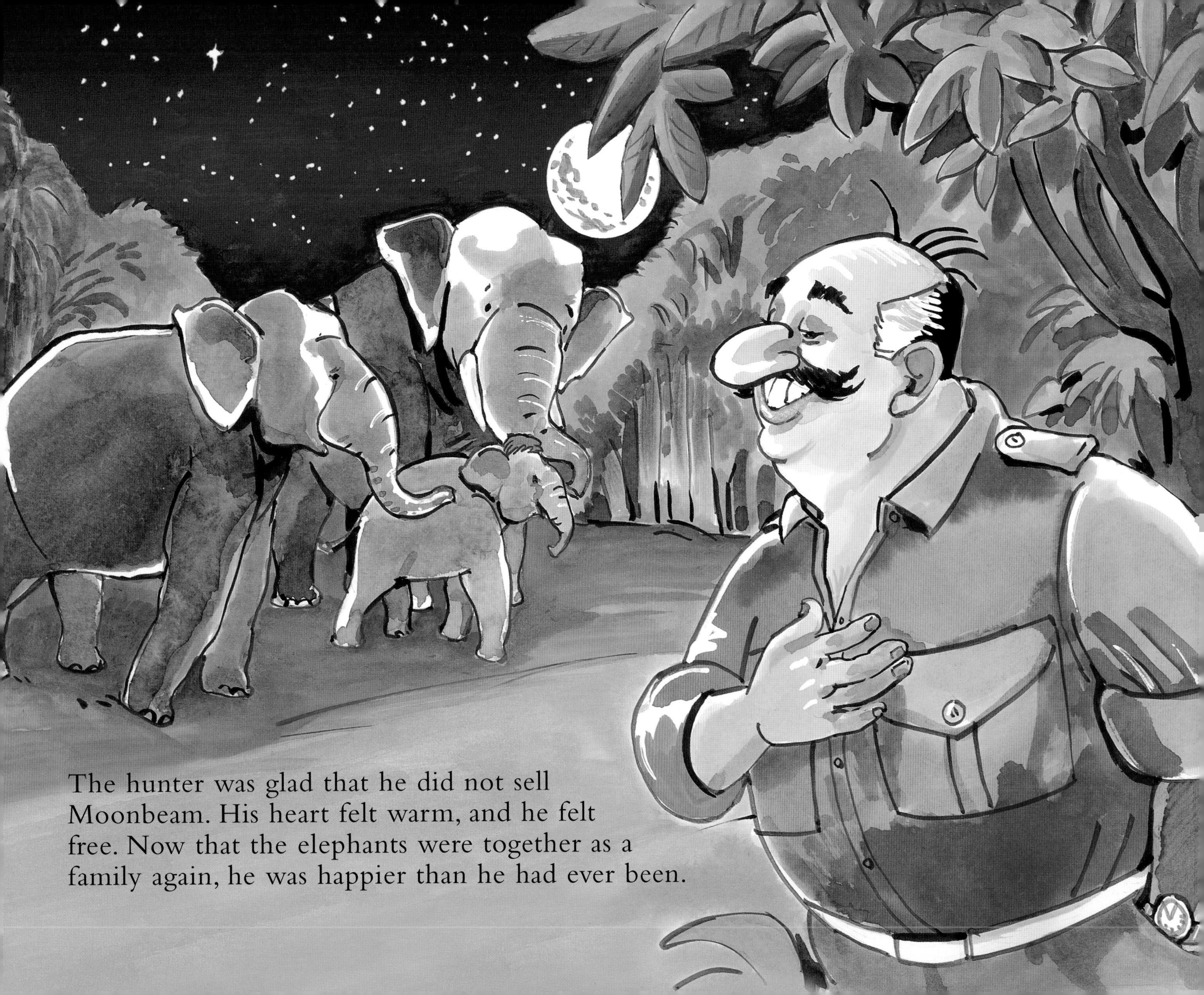

The hunter was glad that he did not sell Moonbeam. His heart felt warm, and he felt free. Now that the elephants were together as a family again, he was happier than he had ever been.

The elephant family was happy.
All the animals, birds, and other creatures in the jungle heard the elephants' loud news and the whole jungle smiled.

He left them to rejoice in their big, beautiful jungle and never set another trap.

Thanks to:
Corey Weinstein, Dave Kendall, David Bergeron, Dave McCoy,
Jason Wayne, Jai Darsi, Michael Ludas, Stephen Welz and Tom Kerr.

Special Thanks to:
C.C. Reddy, T.V. Sri Ramaprasad and Sudheekar Reddy:
without you I could have never produced this wonderful book.

–Sukumar, IDREAM Publications, Inc.

Published by IDREAM Publications, Inc.
Page layout by LunaGraphica.com
Copyright © 2005 All rights reserved.

No part of this publication may be reproduced, stored in a retrieval system, or transmitted in any form, including electronic, mechanical, photocopy, recording, or other means without written permission of the publisher. For information regarding permission, write to: IDREAM Publications, Inc., Attention: Permission Department, 111 Primrose Lane, Wyomissing, PA 19610

Library of Congress Control Number: 2004116996

ISBN 0-9763596-0-X

www.idreampublications.com

Moonbeam–The Little Elephant

First Edition, May 2005

Summary: A greedy hunter captures the baby elephant, Moonbeam, and discovers that helping others in need produces friendship that can break the bonds of captivity.

The artwork was painted with watercolors.

Printed in China